D1516329

DON'T GO IN THERE!

Veronika Martenova Charles

Illustrated by David Parkins

Tundra Books

Published in Canada by Tundra Books,
75 Sherbourne Street, Toronto, Ontario M5A 2P9

Published in the United States by Tundra Books of Northern New York,
P.O. Box 1030, Plattsburgh, New York 12901

Library of Congress Control Number: 2006925075

Library and Archives Canada Cataloguing in Publication

Charles, Veronika Martenova
    Don't go into the forest! / Veronika Martenova Charles ; [illustrated by]
David Parkins.

(Easy-to-read spooky tales)
ISBN 978–0–88776–781–4

    1. Horror tales, Canadian (English). 2. Children's stories, Canadian
(English). I. Parkins, David II. Charles, Veronika Martenova. Easy-to-read
spooky tales. III. Title.

PS8555.H42242D57 2007   jC813'.54   C2006–901942–8

ONTARIO ARTS COUNCIL
CONSEIL DES ARTS DE L'ONTARIO

We acknowledge the financial support of the Government of Canada through the Book
Publishing Industry Development Program (BPIDP) and that of the Government of
Ontario through the Ontario Media Development Corporation's Ontario Book Initiative.
We further acknowledge the support of the Canada Council for the Arts and the Ontario
Arts Council for our publishing program.

Printed and bound in Canada

1 2 3 4 5 6   12 11 10 09 08 07

CONTENTS

CAT-SITTING
PART 1

"Guess what!"

I said to Leon and Marcos.

"I got a job this week,

baby-sitting the cats next door."

"How do you do that?" Leon asked.

"I feed them and clean out

their litter box," I said.

"Can we come too?" Marcos asked.

"Be at my place by five," I told them.

At five o'clock Marcos, Leon, and I

went to my neighbor's house.

"Where are the cats?" Leon asked.

"Outside. They'll come when they

smell their dinner," I said.

I opened three cans of tuna

and put it into three bowls.

Two cats came in through

the screen door.

"Meet Mandy and Fritz," I said.

"We'll have to wait for Blurr."

"Can we look around the house?"

Leon and Marcos asked.

"Sure, just don't go into

that room upstairs," I said.

"How come?" Marcos asked.

"My neighbor just said,

'Don't go in there!' Maybe we

would get trapped like the girl

in a story I know," I replied.

"Tell us that story," said Leon.

TASHA AND THE GOBLIN

(My Story)

Once there was a girl called Tasha

who lived in a village

with her grandparents.

One day, Tasha's friends went

to pick berries in the forest.

"May I go, too?" Tasha asked

her grandma and grandpa.

"You may, but be careful,"

they said. "There's a

goblin's house in the woods.

Don't go in there!"

In the forest, Tasha and her friends

began to pick the berries.

Tasha went from bush to bush,

deeper and deeper into the woods.

When she looked up,

she was all alone.

"How will I get back home?"

Tasha worried.

She walked until she came

to a little house.

The door was open. She went inside.

"Hello, little one," said a goblin

as he locked the door.

"I'm not letting you leave.

From now on, you will

heat my stove and cook my meals."

Tasha cried and cried,

but she did as the goblin said.

One day, Tasha told the goblin,

"I would like to bake some sweets

and take them to my grandparents.

Could I go, for just one day?"

"No," said the goblin.

"I will take them myself."

That's what Tasha wanted.

She baked some pies and

put them in a big wooden box.

Then she said to the goblin,

"Take these to my grandparents

and don't eat any on the way.

I will be watching you.

Now, go and see if it might rain."

When the goblin stepped outside,

Tasha climbed into the box

and covered herself with the pies.

The goblin returned, picked up

the box, and left for the village.

Soon, he grew tired.

"What a heavy box!" he said.

"I'll sit down and eat some pies

to lighten my load."

Tasha called out, "I'm watching you.

Don't eat anything from the box!

Take it to my grandparents."

The goblin was amazed.

Such good eyes she has! he thought.

She can still see me even from there!

He kept walking to the village.

Dogs started to bark in every yard.

The goblin got scared,

dropped the box, and ran back

into the woods.

Tasha's grandparents came out

and saw the box on the road.

"What's in there?" they wondered.

They opened it and saw Tasha.

Everyone was happy

to see each other again.

★   ★   ★

"Leon, what do you think

is in the upstairs room?" I asked.

"Maybe it's a secret room," said Leon.

"Your neighbor goes there

and does things she doesn't want

anyone to see.

I know a story like that.

Listen. . . ."

SALT AND PEPPER

(Leon's Story)

Late one night,

Leroy was coming home

from a party.

He was tired and sleepy

and took a wrong fork

in the road.

He ended up in a swamp.

Leroy couldn't find his way out,

but he saw a light among the trees.

It was coming from a lone cabin.

Leroy went to it and knocked.

An old woman answered the door.

"I'm lost," Leroy said.

"May I stay the night?"

"Come in," the woman said,

and she led him inside.

Even though she was old,

she moved very quickly.

"You can sleep in the kitchen,"

the woman said,

"but don't go in there!"

She pointed to another room.

"I've got work to do

and I don't want to be disturbed."

Leroy lay down,

but noise from that room

kept him awake.

There was stomping, shuffling . . .

What could she be doing in there?

Leroy got up and looked

through the keyhole

into the other room.

The woman was doing a wild dance,

kicking her feet and shaking her body.

All the time she mumbled to herself,

"Too late for dinner,

too early for breakfast,

but tomorrow

I'll turn him into a tasty lunch!"

As the old woman spun around,

her skin slipped off like a dress.

Underneath was a creature

that looked like a giant leopard.

It jumped through

the open window, into the night.

Leroy was scared.

If he escaped now,

the leopard would catch him.

If he stayed, he would be eaten.

How could he save himself?

Leroy grabbed salt and pepper

shakers from the kitchen shelf.

He ran into the other room

and shook them over the skin

that had been left on the floor.

Then he hid in the kitchen closet.

At dawn, Leroy heard screams

coming from that room.

He crept outside and peeked in

through a window.

The creature, now half woman,

half leopard, was rolling

on the ground,

tearing at its own skin.

Here was his chance to get away.

Leroy ran through the swamp

to the fork in the road,

and made his way back home.

"It was smart of Leroy to use
the salt and pepper," I said.
"Once I scraped my knee and then
went swimming in the ocean.
My knee felt like it was on fire
because of the salty water."

"I have a story about a place

you shouldn't go to, also,"

Marcos said. "But first, Leon,

stop that banging!"

"I'm not doing anything," Leon said.

"Well, what's that noise?" Marcos asked.

"What noise? Just tell us the story,"

Leon and I said.

★

WAIT TILL LESTER COMES

(Marcos' Story)

Everybody knew that the house

by the road was haunted.

Alvin passed by it each Sunday

as he went to visit his aunt.

Once, when Alvin was on his way,

the sky suddenly grew dark.

A big storm was coming.

It started to rain.

Alvin took shelter

in that house by the road.

On one of the inside doors,

somebody had painted a sign.

It said: DON'T GO IN THERE!

Why? Alvin wondered.

He peeked in.

There was furniture and a fireplace

with firewood beside it.

Alvin was wet and cold.

He went in and lit a warm fire.

Then he took a book from the shelf,

sat down, and read.

Outside, lighting flashed

and rain pounded the windows.

After a while, Alvin looked up.

A little gray cat was sitting

by the fireplace.

Where did she come from?

Alvin wondered.

Suddenly, the door creaked open
and another cat, big and black,
came inside.

The little gray cat looked at her.

"What should we do with him?"
she asked.

"Wait till Lester comes,"

the big black cat answered.

Alvin pretended not to hear them.

He kept on reading.

Then, the door creaked again.

Another cat, as big as a dog,

came inside.

"What should we do with him?"

asked the little gray cat.

"Wait till Lester comes," answered

the huge cat.

By now, Alvin was scared,

but he pretended not to see them.

Once more, the door creaked.

This time, a gigantic cat,

as big as a cow, came in.

He stopped and stared at Alvin.

"Should we do it now?"

the little gray cat asked.

Alvin didn't wait for the answer.

He dropped the book and ran out

into the raging storm. . . .

CAT-SITTING
PART 2

There was a loud bang.

"Did you hear *that?*" asked Marcos.

"I told you there was banging."

"It came from upstairs," said Leon.

"Probably from that room!

Let's go and see what happened."

I shook my head. "I don't think

we should go in there," I said.

"Maybe we could just look

from the doorway," said Leon.

We went upstairs and looked in.

The room was dark and filled with

old furniture and boxes.

The window was broken.

Something moved inside the room.

BANG!

The chair fell over.

WHOOSH!

Something black and hairy

jumped on us!

"AHHH!" yelled Leon.

"Leopard!" screamed Marcos.

The creature jumped over the railing

and vanished downstairs.

I closed the door fast.

We just stood there and didn't move.

Finally, I tiptoed downstairs.

In the kitchen, Blurr was licking

the last bit of tuna from the bowl.

"Where did you come from?" I asked.

Then it hit me.

"You climbed a tree and went in

through the window, didn't you!"

Leon and Marcos came in next.

"Let me introduce the leopard,

otherwise known as Blurr," I said.

"I knew it was him all along,"

Leon said.

"Me too," said Marcos.

There was another bang upstairs.

"There go the other two.

That must be their playroom.

Let's go home," I said.

We left and locked the door.

On the porch, Mandy, Fritz, and Blurr

were sleeping peacefully.

AFTERWORD

What do *you* think happened

after Alvin left the haunted house

in *Wait Till Lester Comes?*

Did the cats chase after him?

Were the cats *really* cats?

Did Alvin make it to his aunt's house?

Have fun making up your own ending.

WHERE THE STORIES COME FROM

In many folktales from around the world,

the hero is warned not to go into

a particular room, or a certain place.

Of course, the hero always does,

and then strange things happen.

Tasha and the Goblin is from Russia.

Salt and Pepper is based on stories

from the southern United States

and the West Indies. *Wait Till Lester Comes*

is based on an old African-American tale.